MOBY SHINOBI

NINJA ON THE FARM

by Luke Flowers

SCHOLASTIC INC.

FOR GRANDPA BOB

Thanks for training me for life's adventures,
cheering me through wins and failures,
and teaching me to always serve others.
You are my hero. Forever.

Copyright © 2017 by Luke Flowers

Library of Congress Cataloging-in-Publication Data

Names: Flowers, Luke, author, illustrator. Title: Ninja on the farm / by Luke Flowers. Description: New York, NY : Scholastic Inc., 2017. | Series: Scholastic reader. Level 1 | Series: Moby Shinobi ; [1] | Summary: Moby Shinobi wants to put his ninja skills to use by helping a farmer in need, but everything goes wrong until he finds just the right job. Identifiers: LCCN 2016028730| ISBN 9780545935371 (paperback) | ISBN 9780545935388 (hardcover) Subjects: | CYAC: Stories in rhyme. | Ninja—Fiction. | Helpfulness—Fiction. | Farm life—Fiction. | Humorous stories. | BISAC: JUVENILE FICTION / Readers / Beginner. | JUVENILE FICTION / Action & Adventure / General. | JUVENILE FICTION / Animals / Farm Animals. Classification: LCC PZ8.3.F672 Nin 2017 | DDC [E]—dc23 LC record available at https://lccn.loc.gov/2016028730

10 9 8 7 6 5 4 3 2 1   17 18 19 20 21

Printed in Malaysia   108
First printing 2017
Book design by Steve Ponzo

Swoop! Swipe! Snag! I am ninja quick!

Spin! Flip! Whoosh! Watch my super kick!

Run! Jump! Go! I have ninja speed!

Your farm is busy—do not pout!
My ninja skills can help you out.

Farm life starts with a rooster's crow.
Now to the chicken coop we go.

Collect the eggs from every nest.
Be quiet please. They need their rest.

**Moby thinks of how ninjas swoop!
He creeps into the chicken coop.**

Yuck! My coop is covered in goo! Let's find a different job for you.

13

Scoop the hay back into the cart.
The wind is calm, so you should start!

Moby thinks of ninja spin school!
He tries to choose the perfect tool.

Granny's pig pen is extra loud.
Hot, hungry pigs stand in a crowd.

Moby thinks of a ninja jump.
He stands tall on the water pump.

23

Ick! My clothes smell like pigs—PEE-EEW! Maybe farm life is not for you.

The farmer's dog lets out a YELP!
Moby wonders who could need help.

Oh no! My cows broke down the gate! Please save my corn. This cannot wait!

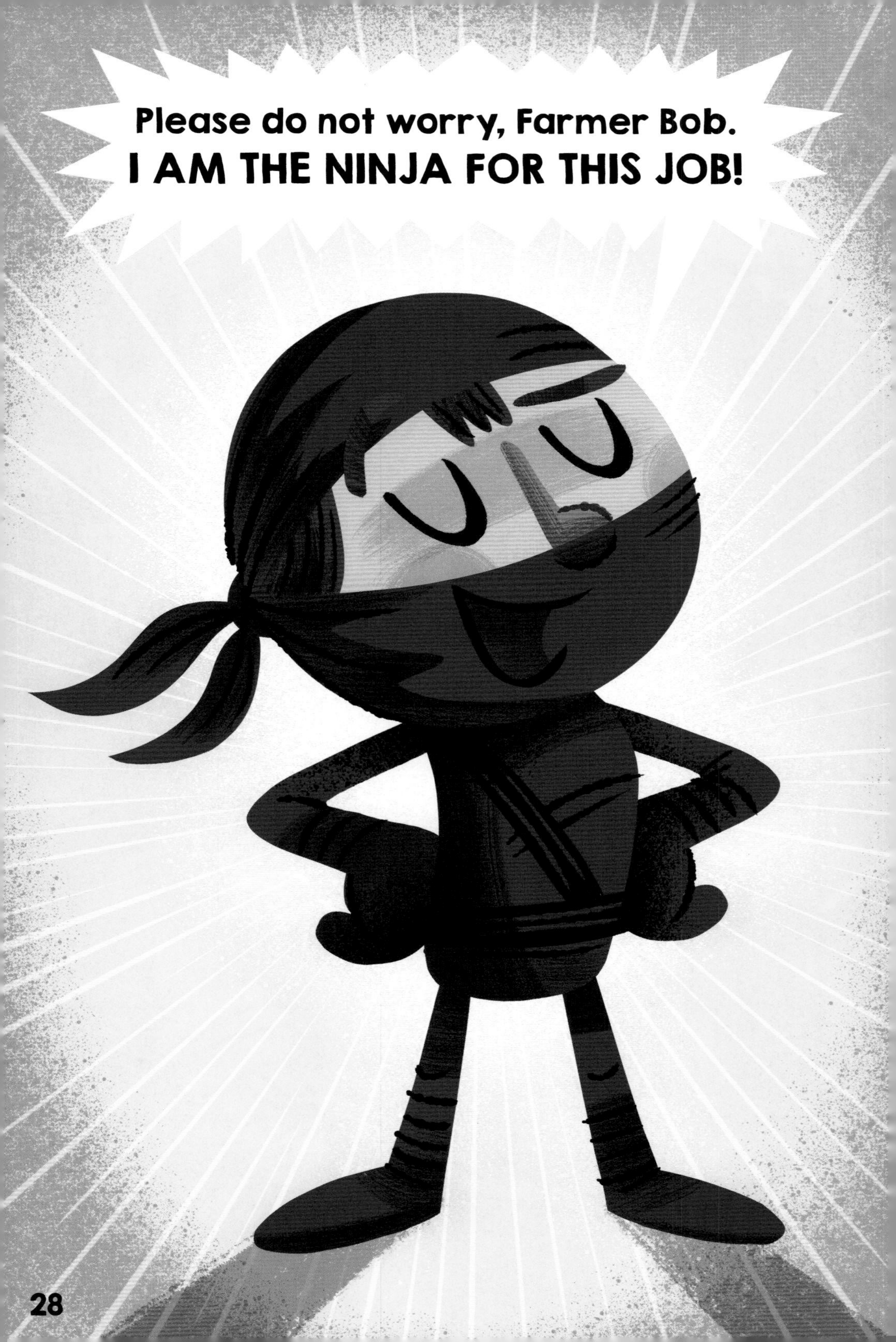
Please do not worry, Farmer Bob.
I AM THE NINJA FOR THIS JOB!

So Moby thinks of rope to throw.
Now it is time to go, go, go!

We thank you for a job well done.
My ninja work has just begun!
PAPA Peppy's
FRESH EGGS